THIS CANDLEWICK BOOK BELONGS TO:

____

____

____

First U.S. paperback edition 2011

The Library of Congress has cataloged the hardcover edition as follows:

Waring, Geoff.
Oscar and the bird : a book about electricity / Geoff Waring.
—1st U.S. ed.
p. cm.
Summary: Oscar the kitten finds a tractor in the field and, when he accidentally turns on the windshield wipers, Bird flies over to answer all his questions about electricity.
ISBN 978-0-7636-4032-3 (hardcover)
[1. Electricity—Fiction. 2. Cats—Fiction. 3. Birds—Fiction. 4. Animals—Infancy—Fiction.] I. Title.
PZ7.W2353Ort 2009
[E]—dc22 2009007351

ISBN 978-0-7636-5302-6 (paperback)

WKT 15 14 13 12 11 10
10 9 8 7 6 5 4 3 2 1

Printed in Shenzhen, Guangdong, China

This book was typeset in ITC Kabel.
The illustrations were created digitally.

Candlewick Press
99 Dover Street
Somerville, Massachusetts 02144

visit us at www.candlewick.com

For Sam, Steph, Paul, Lucy, Martin, Sue, and Helen

The author and publisher would like to thank Sue Ellis at the Centre for Literacy in Primary Education and Martin Jenkins for their invaluable input and guidance during the making of this book.

OSCAR and the BIRD

A BOOK ABOUT ELECTRICITY

Geoff Waring

CANDLEWICK PRESS

One day, Oscar saw a tractor standing in the field. He climbed up to look in the cab, when suddenly the windshield wiper started to move.

Swish, swish!

"How did that happen?" Oscar wondered.

Bird flew down from her branch.
"Electricity is making the wiper move,"
she said. "You must have pressed
the switch by mistake."
"What's electricity?" Oscar asked.
"It's a kind of energy that people use
to help things move, make sounds,
light up, or heat up," Bird said.

"Where does it come from?"
Oscar wanted to know.
Bird hopped down to show
him the engine. "It flows
through wires from this battery,"
she said. "The battery has
chemicals inside it that make
electricity."
"It's a very big battery!" Oscar said.

"It's a big battery for a big tractor," Bird said. "Batteries come in all shapes and sizes—even a tiny one can make electricity."

And she told Oscar about some other machines that are powered by batteries.

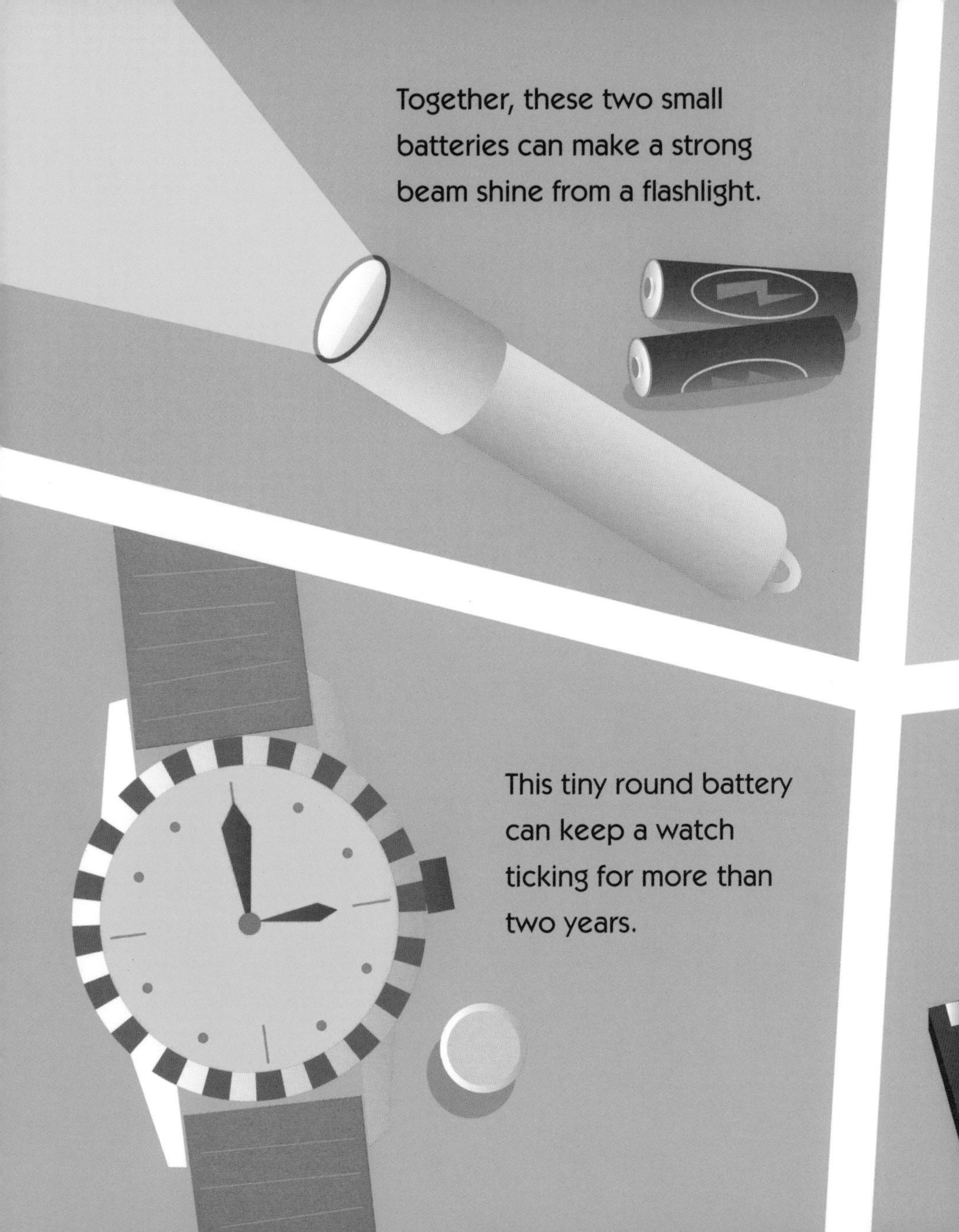

Together, these two small batteries can make a strong beam shine from a flashlight.

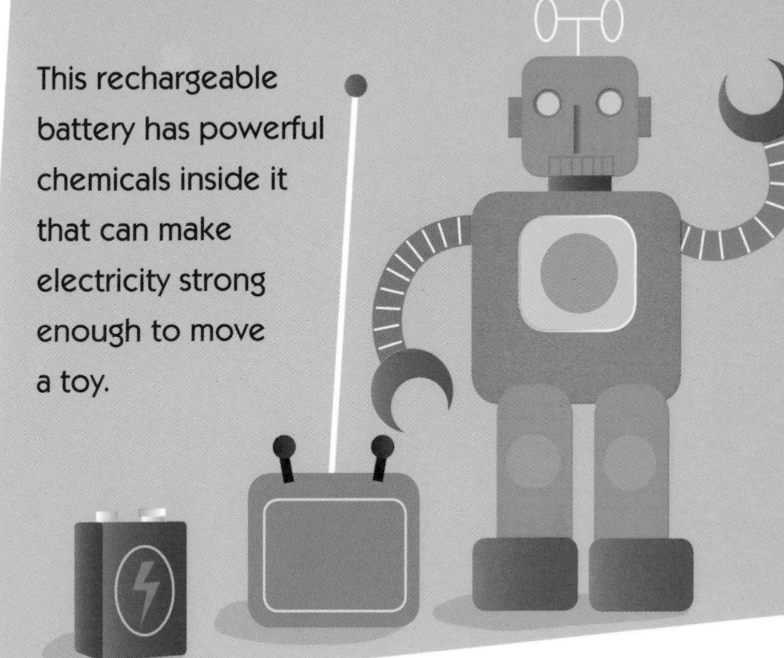

This rechargeable battery has powerful chemicals inside it that can make electricity strong enough to move a toy.

This tiny round battery can keep a watch ticking for more than two years.

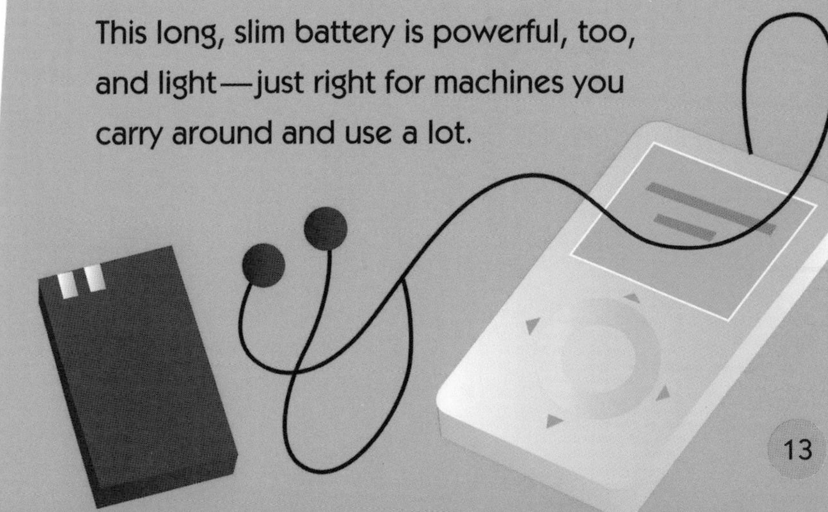

This long, slim battery is powerful, too, and light—just right for machines you carry around and use a lot.

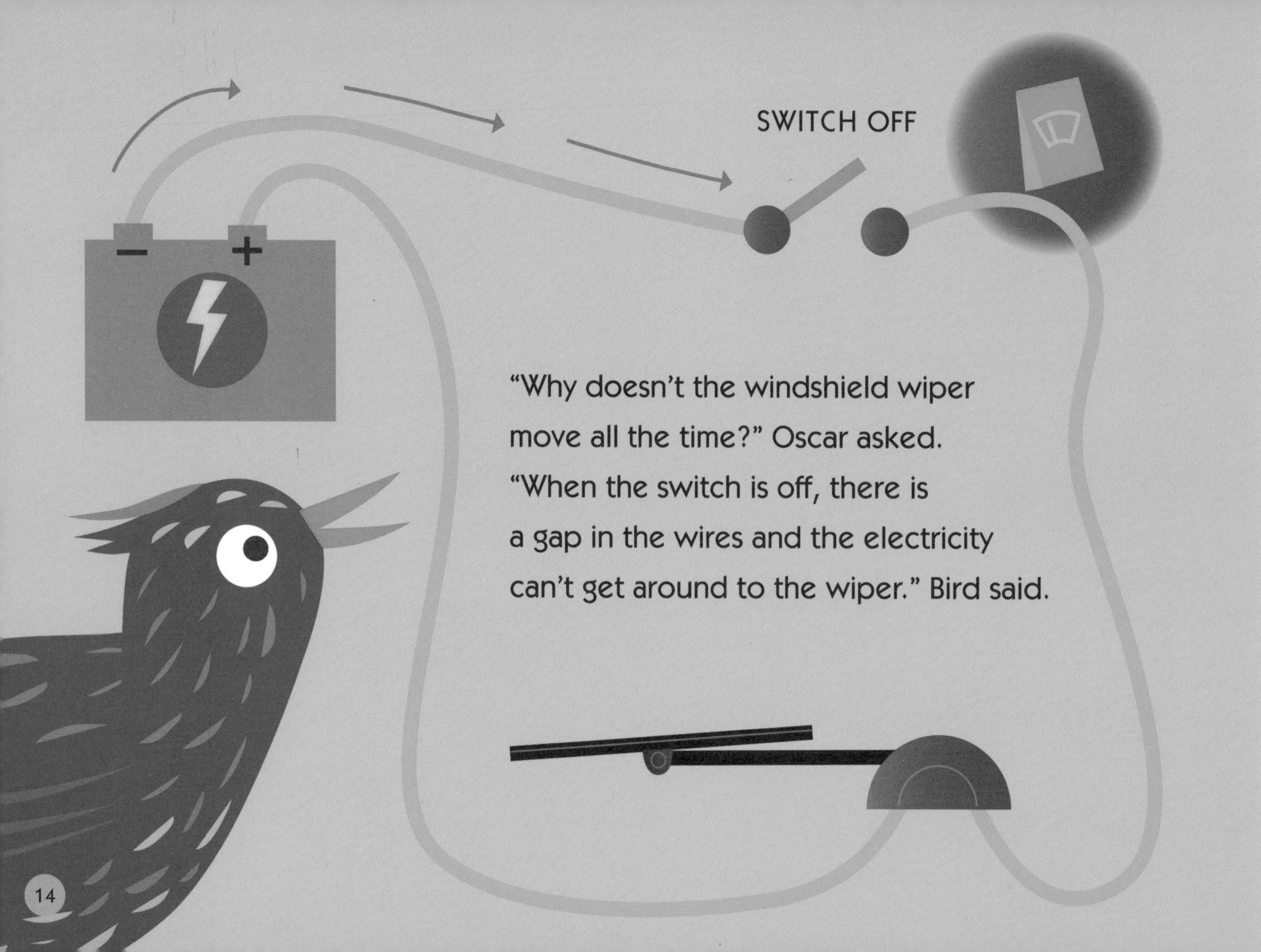

"Why doesn't the windshield wiper move all the time?" Oscar asked. "When the switch is off, there is a gap in the wires and the electricity can't get around to the wiper." Bird said.

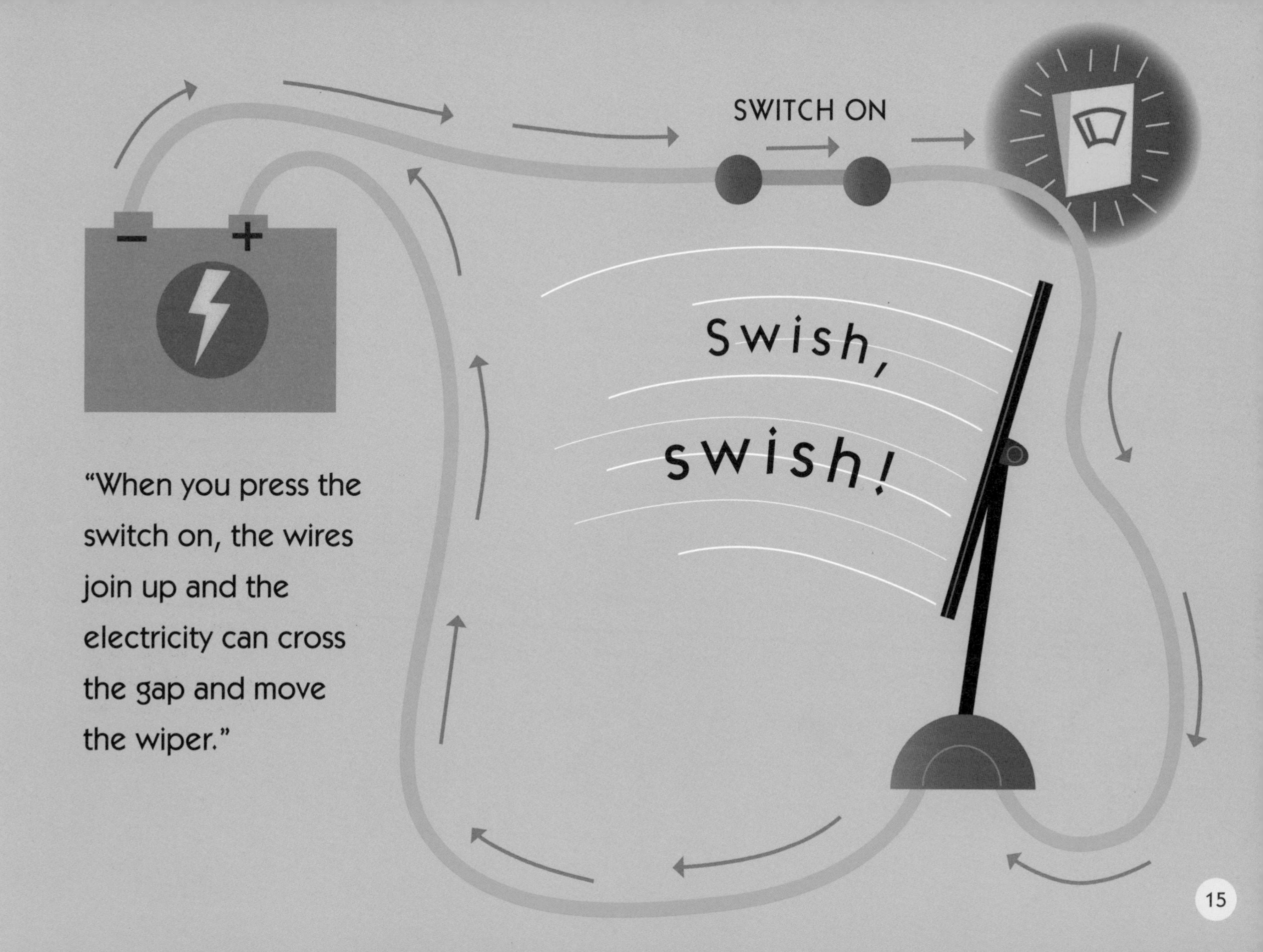

"When you press the switch on, the wires join up and the electricity can cross the gap and move the wiper."

"Does everything in the tractor need electricity to work?" Oscar asked.

"Some things need electricity," said Bird, "like the lights, the radiator, and the wiper. The engine needs electricity to start, too, but it needs gas to make the tractor move."

Oscar looked up.
"Does electricity flow
through those wires
as well?" he asked Bird.
"Yes," Bird answered.

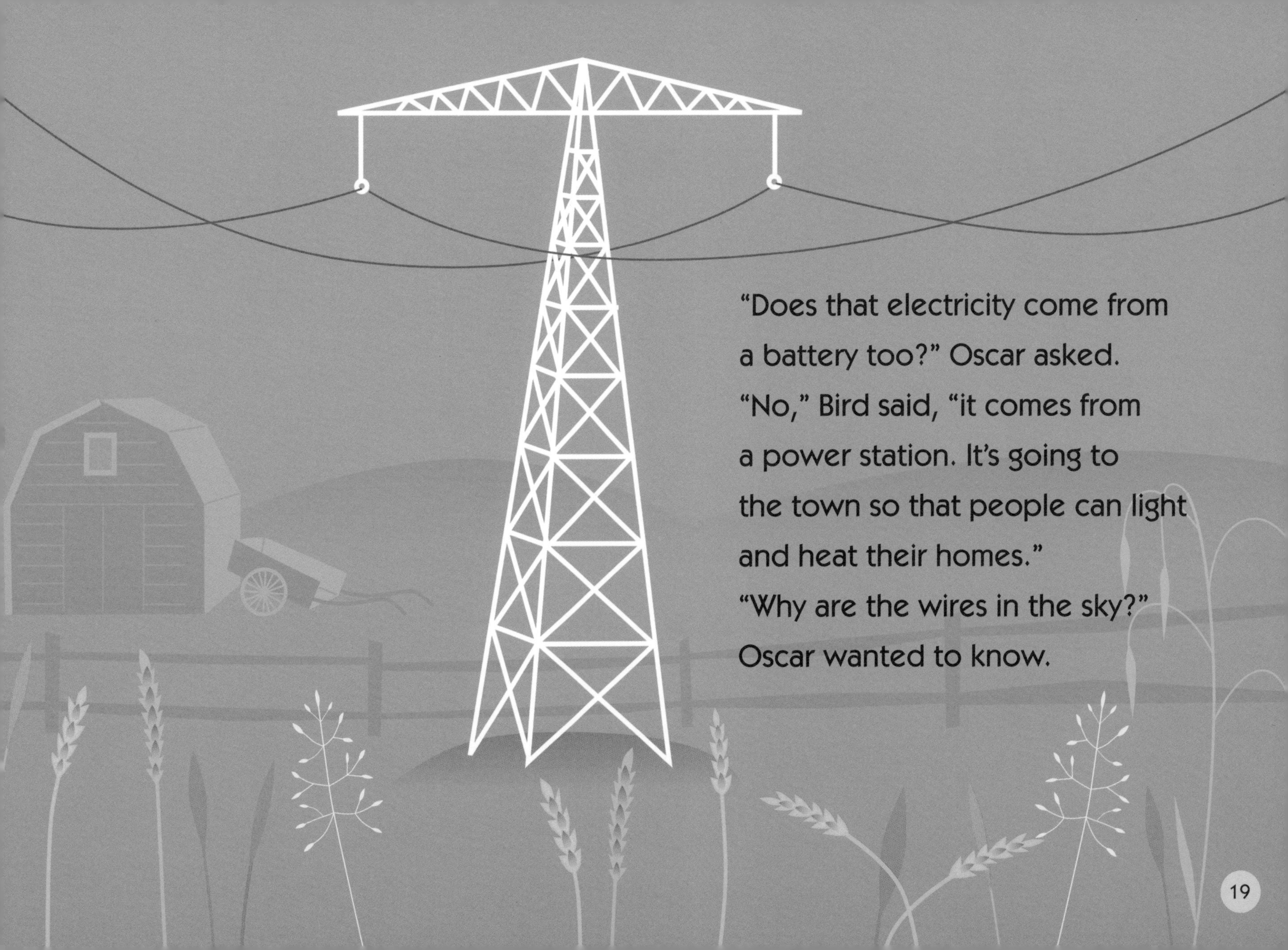

"Does that electricity come from a battery too?" Oscar asked.

"No," Bird said, "it comes from a power station. It's going to the town so that people can light and heat their homes."

"Why are the wires in the sky?" Oscar wanted to know.

"So that they're out of reach and you'll be safer!" Bird said. "They carry LOTS of electricity—and it would be very dangerous if it flowed through you. You should never touch a wire, Oscar."

Just then, in the distance,
they could see flashes of lightning.
“Lightning is electricity too,” Bird said.
“There is a kind of electricity all around us, but
most of the time we don’t see or notice it.”

Over on the hill, the blades on the wind turbines were turning in the wind.

"Is electricity helping them move?" Oscar asked Bird.

"No," Bird said. "It's the other way around! The wind turns the blades, and the movement makes electricity."

Then it started to rain.
Oscar and Bird rushed
back to the tractor.

Swoosh, swoosh!

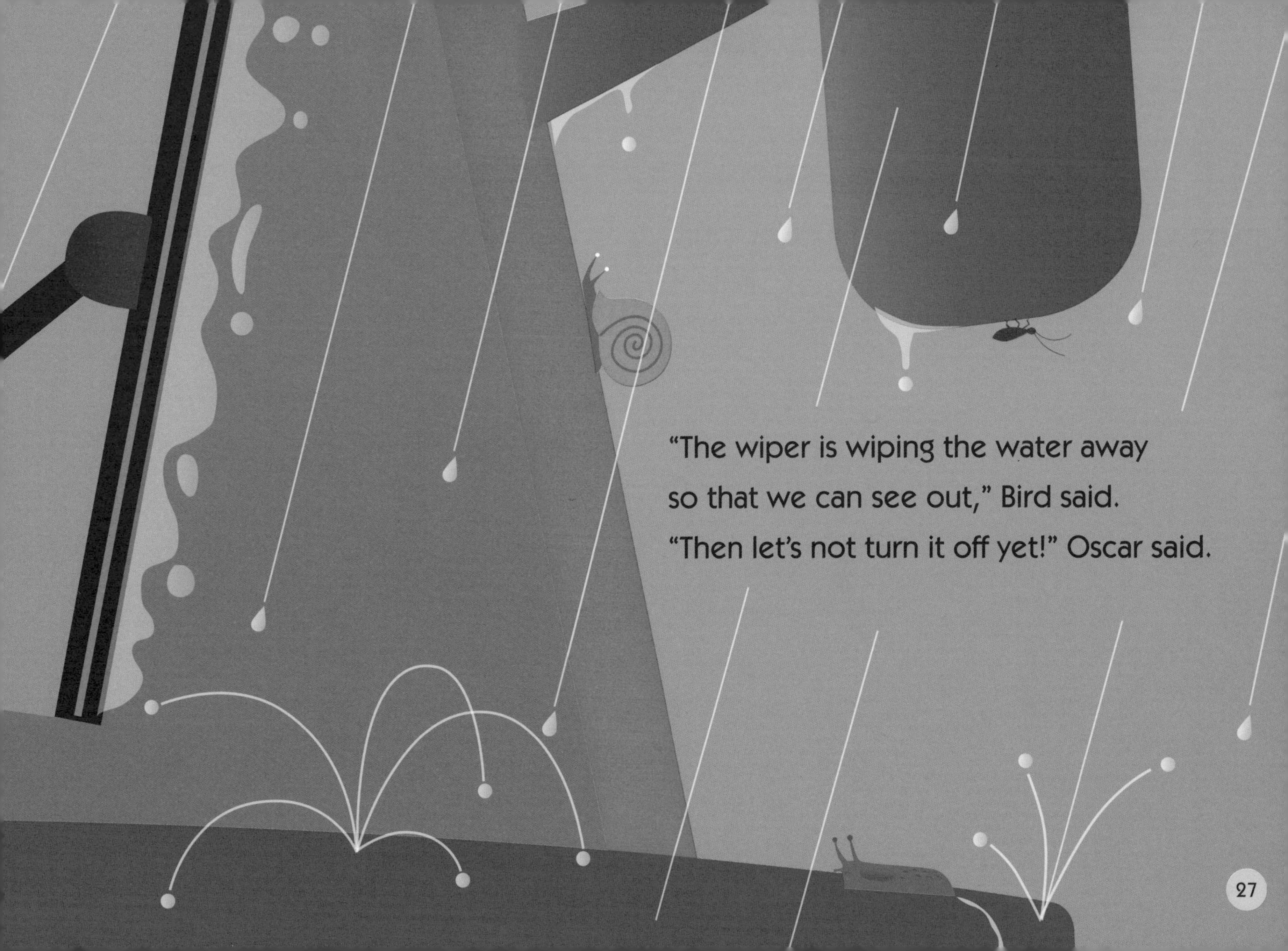

“The wiper is wiping the water away
so that we can see out,” Bird said.
“Then let’s not turn it off yet!” Oscar said.

Thinking about electricity

In the fields, Oscar found out . . .

What electricity is for

Electricity is energy we use as power
to help us do things:

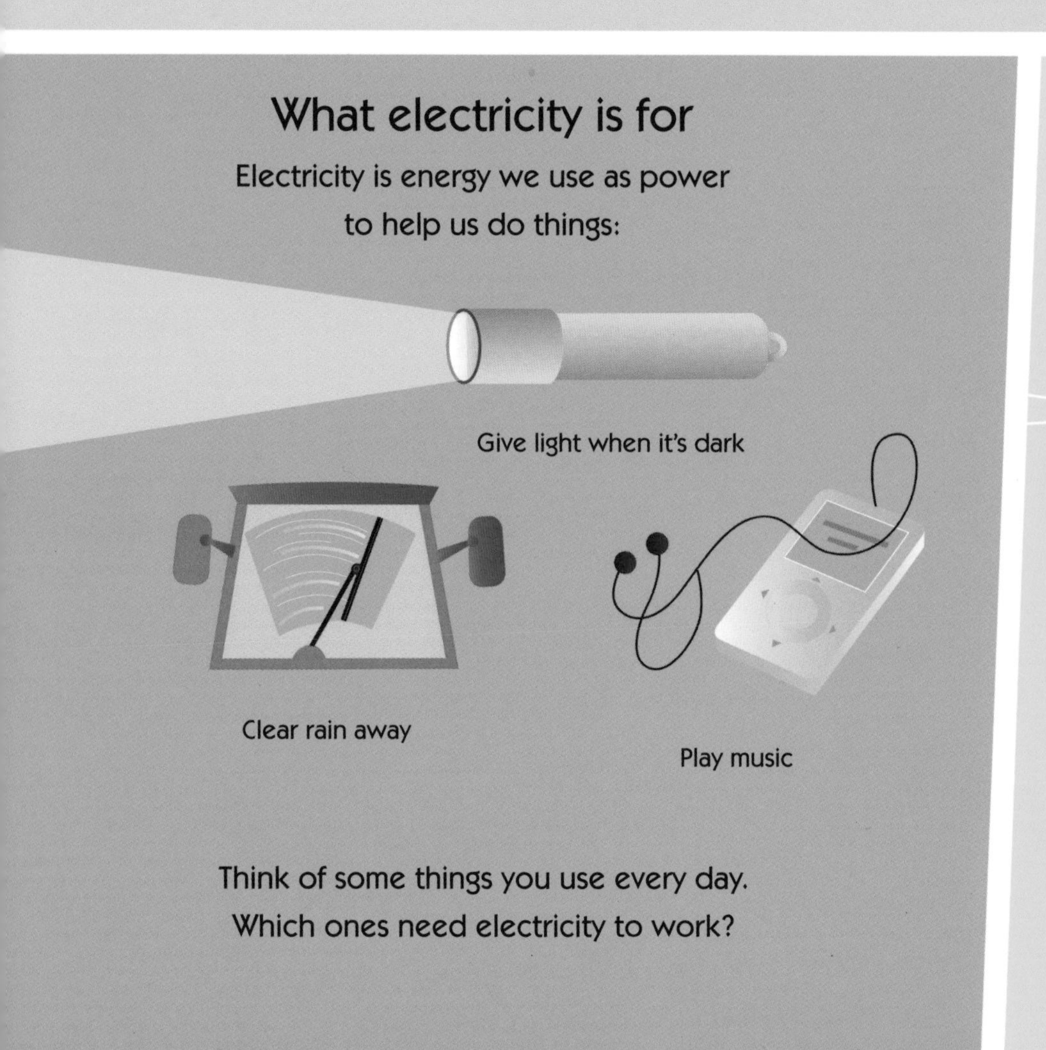

Give light when it's dark

Clear rain away

Play music

Think of some things you use every day.
Which ones need electricity to work?

How electricity works

Electricity flows through wires. The wires are
made of metal to help the electricity flow easily.
Switches can stop or start the flow.

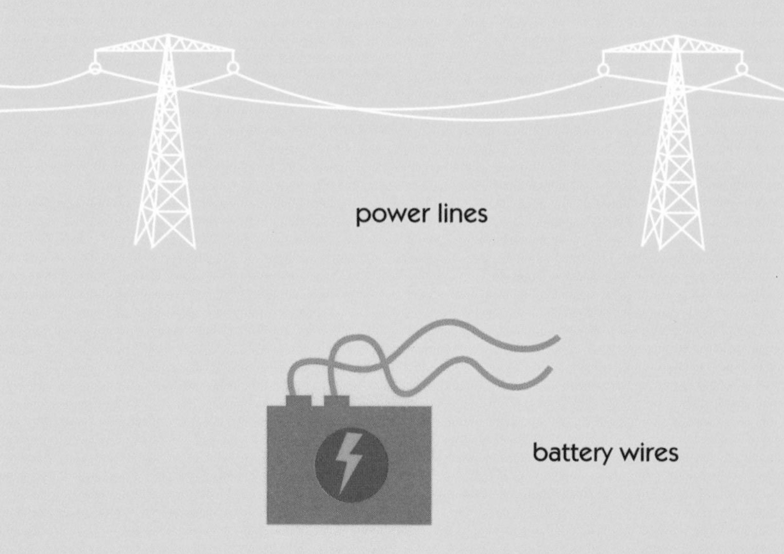

power lines

battery wires

Some electricity is so powerful that it's dangerous.
You should always be careful near wires,
batteries, plugs, and sockets.

What electricity is made from

Electricity is made in different ways:

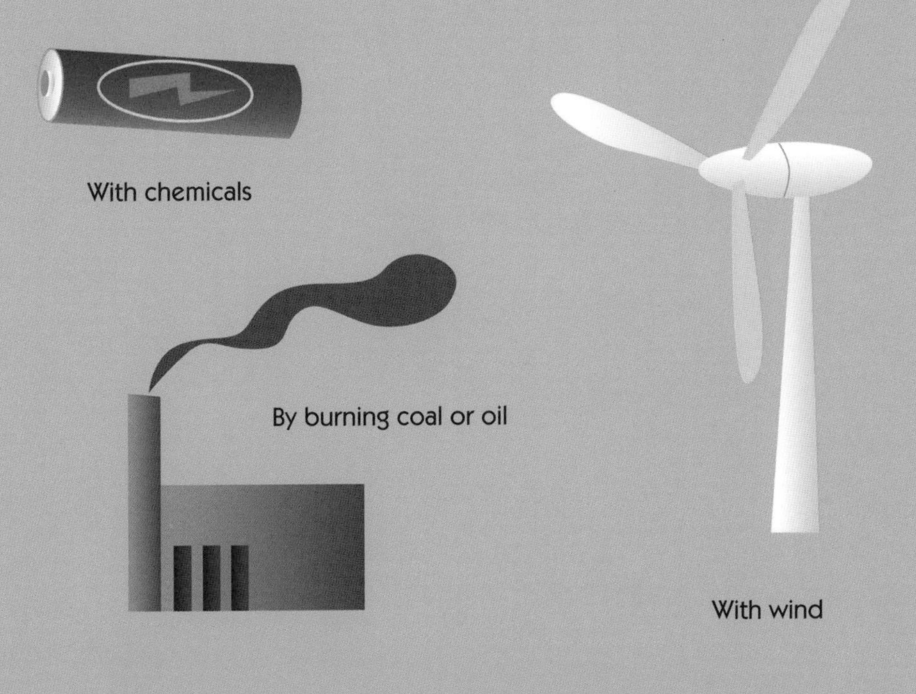

With chemicals

By burning coal or oil

With wind

Lightning is a kind of electricity that is found in nature.

Index

Look up the pages to find out about these electricity things:

Oscar thinks electricity is great! Do you think so, too?

Geoff Waring studied graphics in college and worked as an art director of *British Vogue*. He is currently creative director of *Glamour* magazine. He is the illustrator of *Black Meets White* by Justine Fontes. He says that the Oscar books are based on his own cat, Oskar. Geoff Waring lives in London.